Max Goes to the Moon

A Science Adventure with Max the Dog

Jeffrey Bennett

Illustrated by

Alan Okamoto

Presented by
BIG KID SCIENCE

Editor: Robin J. Heyden
Production: Joan Marsh
Design: Mark Stuart Ong, Side By Side Studios

Published in the United States by
Big Kid Science
3015 Tenth Street
Boulder, Colorado 80304
www.BigKidScience.com

Library of Congress Cataloging in Publication Data
available upon request.

ISBN 0-9721819-0-3

The full-color artwork was prepared using pencil and acrylic paint
on illustration board.

Printed and bound in China

Distributed by Publishers Group West

03   04   05   06   7   6   5   4   3   2   1

Special Thanks to our Scientific and Technical Advisors:

Dr. Thomas R. Ayres, Center for Astrophysics and Space Astronomy,
    University of Colorado, Boulder

Dr. Laura Danly, University of Denver and Denver Museum
    of Nature and Science

Dr. Megan Donahue, Space Telescope Science Institute

Dr. Erica Ellingson, University of Colorado, Boulder

Dr. Cherilynn Morrow, Space Science Institute, Boulder, Colorado

Dr. Nicholas Schneider, University of Colorado, Boulder

Dr. Mark Voit, Space Telescope Science Institute

Dr. James C. White, Rhodes College

Special thanks to Maddy Hemmeter

To Children Around the World:

Follow your dreams, study hard, and someday you'll live in a world
as wonderful as the one we imagine in this book.

3

**T**his is the story of how Max the Dog helped people return to the Moon—this time, to stay.

Phases of the Moon

Do you see the Moon setting over the mountains in the picture of Max's parade? To appreciate what we're seeing, we need to understand the Moon's cycle of phases.

Each cycle takes about a month. That's where the word *month* comes from; think of it as a special way of saying "moonth."

A cycle begins with *new moon*, when we can't see the Moon at all. A couple of days after a new moon, a thin *crescent* ● moon appears in the early evening sky. Then, each day, we see more of the Moon's face and the Moon stays up later at night. About a week after new moon comes *first quarter* ◐ phase, when the Moon shows half its face and stays up until around midnight. A few days later, the Moon's face is bright *except* for a thin, dark crescent; we call this a *gibbous* ◑ (pronounced with a hard *g* as in "gift") moon. *Full moon* ○ comes about two weeks after new moon; we can see the Moon's full face all night long.

After full moon, the Moon goes back through the same phases but with its opposite side illuminated and appearing only later at night. A few days after full moon we have another gibbous moon. ◐ A week after full moon comes *third quarter moon;* ◑ you can't see the third quarter moon at bedtime, because it doesn't rise until around midnight. A few days later, we can see only a thin crescent moon ● in the early morning sky. Then the phases begin again with another new moon. Do you want to know *why* the Moon goes through phases? Try the activity on p. 30.

I t all began on the morning of the parade. Max had just returned from his trip to the Space Station. He was a hero — after all, none of the astronauts could have come home safely without him.

As Max's car drove along Pearl Street, Max looked to the west, and he began to howl just as the Moon set over the mountains.

In truth, Max howled because he heard a siren. He always howls at sirens. But the TV reporters didn't know that, so they thought he was howling at the Moon.

A reporter spotted Max's friend, Tori.

"Why did Max howl at the Moon?," he asked.

"I'm not sure," said Tori. "Maybe it's because he wants to go there."

The Moon in the Daytime

Children's stories often make it seem like the Moon and bedtime always go together. But there are many nights when we cannot see the Moon at bedtime and many days when we can see it in the daytime sky.

Each day, the Moon rises in the east and sets in the west much like the Sun. The times of moonrise and moonset depend on the Moon's phase.

A new moon rises and sets with the Sun, which is why we cannot see it at all: in the daytime it is hidden in the Sun's glare and at night it is below our horizon. As the phases progress from new to full — which we call the "waxing" (getting fuller) phases — the Moon rises and sets later and later compared to the Sun. A waxing crescent moon trails a couple of hours behind the Sun in the sky, making it visible in the late afternoon and early evening. A first quarter moon rises around noon and sets around midnight, making it visible for much of the afternoon and all of the evening. A full moon rises and sets opposite the Sun, keeping it above the horizon all night long.

The pattern continues with the "waning" (getting less full) phases. For example, a waning gibbous moon rises a few hours after sunset and sets a few hours after sunrise, while a third quarter moon rises around midnight and sets around noon. If you look closely, you'll see that it is a waning gibbous moon over Max's parade, which is why it is visible in the mid-morning sky.

Many newspapers show the Moon's daily phase and times of moonrise and moonset.

Leaving the Earth

If you throw a ball into the air, it falls back to the ground. But the harder and faster you throw it upward, the higher it goes before coming down. If you had magical strength, you could throw a ball so hard and so fast that it would never come back down. We would say that you gave the ball *escape speed*, because it went upward fast enough to escape from the Earth and go out into space.

The escape speed from the Earth is very fast — about 25,000 miles per hour (40,000 kilometers per hour). That is much faster than anyone can really throw a ball. It is faster than any airplane travels. But big rockets can go that fast.

Well, Tori's "maybe" was good enough for TV. By the next day, Max's dream of going to the Moon was all over the news. And because no one had been to the Moon in a long time, it seemed like it was about time for someone—or some dog—to go.

DAILY WORLD NEWS

MOON-DOGGY DOG

MOON

$.25

K-9 COURAGE

NASA

It's not easy to go to the Moon. It takes big rocket engines to get a spaceship off the Earth. It takes careful planning to make sure the astronauts reach the Moon and come back safely. And it costs a lot of money.

But everywhere Max went, crowds chanted, "Send Max to the Moon!" People wrote letters to the President. So a new moonship was built and assembled at the Space Station.

A Trip to the Moon

Past Moon missions took astronauts directly from the Earth to the Moon with big, multi-stage rockets. Future Moon missions may include a stop at the Space Station. (The Space Station will require modifications in order to support a Moon mission.)

The Space Station makes Moon trips easier in two ways. First, it makes it easier to put a large moonship in orbit. Without the Station, we'd need a huge rocket to get the moonship into space. With it, we can use smaller rockets to launch the moonship in pieces, then assemble the pieces at the Station.

Second, starting from the Station gives the moonship a head start on achieving escape speed. The Space Station orbits about 250 miles (400 km) above the Earth at a speed of about 17,000 miles per hour (27,000 kilometers per hour). Thus, a moonship docked at the Space Station already is traveling this fast, so its engines need only to boost it an additional 8,000 miles per hour (13,000 kilometers per hour) to reach escape speed.

9

Tori gave Max the good news. "You are going to go to the Moon," she said. "I sure hope they let me come with you."

Why Is the Moon a "moon"?

Our Moon is a "moon" because it orbits the Earth. Planets orbit the Sun, and there are nine planets in our solar system: Mercury, Venus, Earth, Mars, Jupiter, Saturn, Uranus, Neptune, and Pluto. Moons orbit planets, and there are dozens of moons in our solar system. Mercury and Venus are the only planets with no moons at all.

The Moon is about 2,160 miles (3476 kilometers) in diameter, which is a little more than one-fourth of the Earth's diameter. The Moon's average distance from Earth is about 239,000 miles (384,000 kilometers). The photographs below of the Earth and Moon show their relative sizes to scale. If you wanted to show the distance between them on the same scale, you'd need to hold these two pictures about 1.9 meters (6 feet, 3 inches) apart.

Max went into astronaut training again. The other astronauts were glad to have Max back. Max made the long training sessions seem fun.

Somehow, he always managed to find a stick. He loved to play fetch while the astronauts trained in the water tank. He also loved to play tug-o-war—and guess who always won?

The Face of the Moon

The Moon always shows nearly the same face to Earth, so no one ever saw the Moon's back side, or "far side," until we sent space probes to photograph it.

What some people call the "man in the moon" is just a pattern of large craters and *maria* that we see on the Moon's face. Craters are scars from impacts of asteroids and comets. The maria are located at the sites of especially large impacts — so large that they fractured the Moon's surface. Molten lava later rose up through the cracks and filled these huge craters, leaving a smooth surface when it cooled and solidified.

By the way, the word *maria* is Latin for "seas"; they got their name because their smooth appearance reminded ancient people of the smooth surfaces of oceans seen from afar.

maria

Apollo and Beyond

The scene on these pages shows Apollo 11 on the Moon in July 1969. Astronauts must wear spacesuits on the Moon, because the Moon has no air. Of course, no air also means no wind. So why does the flag look like it's blowing in the wind? It's because the flag is made of foil. With no wind or air, the foil holds the shape it had when the astronauts unfurled it.

The Apollo 11 astronauts spent less than 24 hours on the Moon. Their entire trip from the Earth to the Moon and back took about eight days.

Five more Apollo missions landed on the Moon over the next three years — Apollo 12, 14, 15, 16, and 17. (Apollo 13 had an accident while in space. It did not land on the Moon, but the astronauts returned home safely.) The last Apollo mission was in December 1972, and no one has been to the Moon since.

The Apollo missions were run by NASA — the *National Aeronautics and Space Administration* of the United States. NASA is still a leader in most space missions, including the international Space Station. But today, NASA usually works with partners from around the world, including the Canadian Space Agency, the Japanese Space Agency, and the European Space Agency (ESA). Many other nations also have space agencies, and astronauts, space scientists, and space engineers come from almost every nation on Earth.

Tori thought that Max should know a little history before his trip. So she told Max about the first astronauts who went to the Moon.

"Listen carefully, Max. Neil Armstrong and Buzz Aldrin were the first people to walk on the Moon. Their mission was called Apollo 11. They landed on the Moon on July 20, 1969. Neil Armstrong stepped out first. Do you know what he said when he took his first moon step?"

"Armstrong said:

That's one small step for a man,
one giant leap for mankind.

"Do you understand, Max?"
Max barked, and Tori took that as a "yes."
"Good boy, Max," said Tori.

NASA chose six experienced astronauts to go to the Moon with Max. Since Max and Tori made such a good team, Tori got to go along too.

So the crew of seven humans and one dog blasted off into space.

Wings in Space?

Airplanes and rockets both fly, but in very different ways. Airplanes need wings to fly. Airplane wings have special shapes so that, when the airplane goes fast enough, air pushes up under the wings harder than it pushes down over them. The extra upward push creates what we call *lift*, allowing the airplane to fly. Pilots can adjust flaps on the wings to increase or decrease the lift, making the plane go up or down.

Wings are useless in space, because there is no air to provide lift. That is why space-ships need rocket engines. (The Space Shuttle uses its wings only for landing on Earth.)

Within a few hours, they were docked at the Space Station, where their moonship was waiting. After lunch on the Space Station, the crew boarded the moonship.

The crew fired the moonship's rocket engines to gain speed, leaving Earth orbit. Once on their way, they turned off the engines and coasted toward the Moon. The trip took a little more than two days.

A rocket works by shooting a stream of hot gas out its back, which makes the rocket itself go forward. It's the same basic idea as when you inflate a balloon and let it go without tying the end: the balloon flies forward as air shoots out its end. Of course, the rocket engine offers much more power and much more control than the balloon.

It may look like rockets "push off" the ground, but they don't; their power comes from shooting the hot gas out the back. In fact, the ground (and air in our atmosphere) gets in the way of the streaming gas, so rocket engines perform better in space than on Earth.

Amazingly, spaceships don't even need rocket engines, except to speed up, slow down, or turn. In space, where there's no air to create friction or drag, spaceships can coast forever without engine power. That's why the moonship can cut its engines once on its way to the Moon. It's also why spaceships and satellites don't need fuel to remain in orbit around the Earth, as long as their orbits are high enough to be fully above the Earth's atmosphere.

The same idea explains why the Moon needs no fuel to keep orbiting the Earth and why the Earth and other planets need no fuel to keep orbiting the Sun. With no air to slow them down, moons and planets can orbit forever.

Soon, the Moon loomed large in the window, with the Earth far behind. The crew turned the ship around, so firing the rocket engines slowed it down. As the moonship neared the surface, the blast from its engines kicked up a cloud of moon dust. Then it settled gently onto the Moon.

15

Spacesuits

You probably know that spacesuits allow astronauts to carry air with them. But did you ever wonder why spacesuits are so thick?

One reason is to protect astronauts from temperature extremes. With no air to moderate temperatures in space, it gets very hot in sunlight and very cold in shadow — the difference from light to shadow on the Moon can be 400°F (220°C)! Spacesuits must have heating and cooling systems to keep temperatures steady for the astronauts inside.

A second reason is to protect astronauts from dangerous radiation from the Sun, such as ultraviolet and X rays. On Earth, our atmosphere protects us from this radiation. In space, astronauts outside their spaceships must rely on their spacesuits to block this radiation. Protection from radiation is also why astronauts have dark, coated visors on their helmets; we've taken artistic license in this book so you can see faces behind the visors.

Spacesuits also allow astronauts to communicate, because they contain built-in radios. Despite what you may have heard in science fiction movies, sound cannot travel through empty space. Space is always silent, and even explosions make no sound in space. When we hear astronauts talking in space, we are actually hearing voices transmitted by the radios in their spacesuits.

Max was so excited about reaching the Moon that the crew had a hard time getting his spacesuit on. It took three of them just to hold Max while the others pulled the spacesuit over his legs. Tori made sure that Max's tail went in the right place. Then they closed all the buckles and attached his helmet. Finally, they checked carefully to make sure that the spacesuit was airtight.

When they opened the airlock, Max jumped out. You should have seen the look on his face! He went much higher and farther than he had expected. It also took him much longer to come down than he was used to on Earth. Tori watched out the window and said,

"That's one giant leap for a dog!"

Weak Gravity

Have you ever wondered *why* objects fall to the ground? The answer is gravity, which pulls everything on Earth downward. If you jump up, gravity pulls you back down. It keeps pulling even when you are on the ground, which is what gives you weight.

On Earth, the strength of gravity is about the same everywhere. But gravity is different on other worlds. Gravity on the Moon is about six times weaker than on the Earth, so you would weigh only about one-sixth as much on the Moon as you do on Earth. Everything else weighs less on the Moon too, so you could lift big objects that would be too heavy to lift on Earth, and throw things much higher and farther.

The Moon's weaker gravity also means that everything falls back to the ground more slowly than it does on Earth. That, along with reduced weight, is why astronauts find it easier to bound than to walk on the Moon. It is also why Max got such a big surprise when he made his first Moon leap.

The Airless Moon

Max noticed a lot of strange things on the Moon, many of which occur because the Moon has no atmosphere. That's why astronauts (and astrodogs!) must bring their own air with them in their spaceships and spacesuits, and why their spacesuits must protect them from dangerous radiation. But the lack of air has other effects too.

On Earth, the atmosphere creates *pressure*, without which the oceans would boil even at low temperatures. The Moon's lack of atmosphere means no pressure and therefore no liquid water. With no air and no liquid water, there is no life on the Moon. That's why Max could not find any sticks.

On Earth, wind and rain cause *erosion* that usually erases footprints within a few days. There is no wind or rain on the Moon, which is why astronaut footprints — and Max's paw prints — can remain unchanged for centuries.

On Earth, air holds warmth and spreads sunlight into shadows. Because there is no air on the Moon, the shadows are extremely cold and dark. That's why Max couldn't see anything and his head got very cold when he looked into the shadow behind a rock.

On Earth, the atmosphere spreads the Sun's light all over the sky, making the daytime sky bright and blue and hiding the dim light of stars. On the Moon, the lack of air means the sky is blacker than the darkest night. If you look away from the Sun and the bright lunar surface, you can see stars even in the daytime on the Moon.

For posterity, the astronauts fenced off the spot where Max made his first paw prints on the Moon. There is no wind or rain on the Moon, so those paw prints are still there today, even though it has been many years since Max's first Moon trip.

Max thought it would be fun to play with a stick. He didn't see any, so he decided to look behind a big rock. But when he poked his head into the rock's shadow, he couldn't see a thing. It was darker than the darkest night, and cold, too.

(using a technique called radiometric dating), shows that they formed about 4.6 billion years ago. So our solar system must be 4.6 billion years old. Similar studies of Earth rocks allow scientists to learn about the Earth's past history.

No one is quite sure how the Moon formed, though many scientists suspect it was made after a gigantic asteroid slammed into the young Earth. The collision blasted much of the Earth's outer layers into Earth orbit. Gravity then pulled this orbiting material together to make the Moon. If this really is how the Moon formed, then the Moon is made entirely of rock that was once part of the Earth. Studies of moon rocks brought back by the Apollo astronauts strongly support this idea of how the Moon formed, though we may never have absolute proof that it is correct.

Falling Without Air

Tori's demonstration with the feather and rock reveals an important fact about gravity: without air to affect motion, all objects would fall to the ground at the same rate.

This fact surprises many people, because on Earth we are always surrounded by air. Indeed, this fact about gravity was discovered only about 400 years ago, by the famous Italian scientist named Galileo.

You can test this fact for yourself. If you drop a rock and a flat piece of paper, the rock falls rapidly while the paper wafts gently to the ground. But if you wad the paper into a tight ball, so that air cannot affect it so much, the rock and the ball of paper fall together.

Tori picked up the Frisbee and threw it again. This time Max knew what to do. She threw it very high, so Max had time to get under it. He stopped and turned around to see the Frisbee coming down. He was perfectly positioned for the catch.

There was only one problem...

Frisbees and Curve Balls on the Moon

The effects of air are even more dramatic for Frisbees and other flying toys. Their fancy curves and turns are possible only because of the way air pushes against them. Without air, a Frisbee's path through the sky would be as simple as the path of a thrown rock. That's why Max was surprised by Tori's first throw; he expected it to curve like it would have on Earth.

Air swirling around a fast-moving baseball is also what makes curve balls possible. Outside on the Moon, even the best major league pitcher would have no curve ball.

Of course, if you played inside an air-filled Moon colony, Frisbees and baseballs would behave as they do on Earth — except they could be thrown higher and farther and would remain airborne longer.

Max, Tori, and the astronauts had plenty of work to do for the next few days. They collected moon rocks for science, and they set up telescopes to study distant planets and stars. But most of all, they loved gazing upward at the Earth, which seemed to hang in one place in the sky.

Soon, the longer shadows told Max and the crew that darkness was coming. It was time to leave.

Once everyone was aboard the moonship, Max and Tori waved goodbye to the Moon, and the crew closed the door. They fired the rocket engines and blasted off the Moon.

Just twelve days after leaving the Earth, Max, Tori, and the rest of the astronauts were back on the Space Station. Then a Space Shuttle took them home.

Day and Night on the Moon

We have day and night because the Earth spins, or *rotates*, once each day.

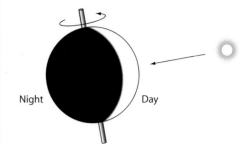

Night   Day

The Moon rotates too, but more slowly: the Moon's "day" lasts about a month instead of 24 hours. On the Moon, you'd have about two weeks from sunrise to sunset, followed by two weeks of night.

The Moon's rotation is special in another way: it is just the right speed so that the Moon always keeps the same face toward Earth. This special rotation is not a coincidence; it is a natural consequence of the way gravity affects the Earth and Moon. Looking from the Moon's surface, the Earth would seem to hang in your sky, always in about the same place and neither rising nor setting. But as it hangs in the sky, you'd see the Earth go through a monthly cycle of phases, from new to full and back again, just as we see phases of the Moon from Earth. You'd also see the Earth slowly rotating, completing a full turn once every 24 hours.

Back on Earth, billions of people watched Max's trip on the news. Everyone talked about it. Some grownups said the trip wasn't worth the money it cost.

Why Build a Moon Colony?

A Moon colony would be a great place to visit, with beautiful views and the fun of playing in weak gravity. But a Moon colony could also offer practical benefits to people.

We could mine rocks from the Moon, sending them to Earth or using them to build Moon colonies and spaceships for exploring the rest of the solar system.

Mining the Moon might also give us an almost endless supply of energy for Earth. The Moon's soil contains a trapped gas, called helium-3, which is very rare on Earth. Some scientists believe this gas could be used as fuel for power plants that would generate energy (by nuclear fusion) with little pollution or radioactive waste.

But astronomy may be the best reason for building a Moon colony. Thanks to the Moon's lack of air, telescopes on the Moon would have a clearer view of the universe than telescopes on Earth.

But children understood the excitement of it all. They asked their parents to help send Max to the Moon again — but this time to build a big colony where many children could go visit him and learn about the universe.

Atmospheres and Telescopes

We depend on Earth's atmosphere for survival, but the atmosphere creates two major problems for telescopes.

First, do you remember the song *Twinkle, Twinkle, Little Star*? Twinkling may be beautiful, but it blurs pictures taken with telescopes on Earth. To understand why, drop a coin to the bottom of a glass of water. Stir up the water and the coin will look like it is moving, because you are looking at it through moving water. In much the same way, we see stars twinkle only because we view them through the moving air in the Earth's atmosphere. Viewed from space, starlight is steady as can be.

To understand the second problem, think about a dog whistle. Dogs can hear it, but people can't. Just as there are sounds we cannot hear, there are some kinds of light we cannot see. However, we can still make pictures from this light by using special telescopes and cameras. The pictures show us what things would look like *if* our eyes could see this light. These special pictures can reveal details about the universe that would otherwise remain invisible. The Earth's atmosphere blocks most of the invisible light, so we can study it only with telescopes in space or on the Moon.

Visible light

Radio waves   Infrared   Ultraviolet   X Rays   Gamma rays

← Different forms of light →

25

The children were so convincing that all the nations of the world decided to work together to build a big, domed colony on the Moon.

The domes covered homes, offices, and, of course, the University of the Moon. They were filled with air so that no one needed a spacesuit inside. Food grew in greenhouses and water was carefully recycled.

Outside the domes, astronauts built great telescopes to observe the universe. Students and scientists made important new discoveries almost every day.

Space Telescopes and Moon Telescopes

Putting telescopes above the Earth's atmosphere solves the problems of twinkling and of studying invisible light. That is why many powerful telescopes are already in Earth orbit. For example, the Hubble Space Telescope views the universe without the blurring caused by twinkling, and the Chandra X-Ray Observatory studies X-rays that cannot be seen from the ground on Earth.

Telescopes on the Moon won't see any better than telescopes in space, but the Moon's solid surface will make them easier for astronauts to build and operate. It's much easier to work while standing than while floating weightlessly in space. The bigger the telescopes, the greater the advantages of working on the Moon. Someday, we may have a great lunar observatory that will teach us much more about the universe and how we came to exist within it.

The building of the Moon Colony also changed a lot of things back on Earth.

Children tried to learn more in school, in hopes that they might get to attend the University of the Moon. Grownups saved their money for tourist trips to the Moon.

Most importantly, the beautiful views of Earth from the Moon made everyone realize that we all share a small and precious planet.

Of course, none of it would have happened without Max.
Max was glad that he had been so helpful. But he was not the
type of dog to stop at that.

It's a big universe out there. Where would he go next?

Understanding the Phases of the Moon

Do you want to know why the Moon goes through phases? It's easy to understand with a simple demonstration.

Take a ball outside on a sunny day, and pretend the ball is the Moon. Pretend your head is the Earth. Hold the ball at arm's length and spin slowly around (always turning to your left), so that the ball goes around you just like the Moon orbits around the Earth. Although the half of the ball facing the Sun is always sunlit and the other half is always dark, the face of the ball that *you* see will go through phases as you turn.

Start by holding the ball toward the Sun. You'll see only the dark half of the ball, so this represents "new ball." As you begin to turn, you'll see the ball go through waxing phases. First, you'll see a sunlit crescent. Then, when you've made a quarter turn, you'll see a face of the ball that is half sunlit and half dark. We call this "first quarter" phase because the ball has gone one-quarter of the way around a circle. Next, you'll see a "gibbous ball" with more than half its face in sunlight. After half a spin, you'll have your back to the Sun and you'll see "full ball."

As you continue to turn after full ball, you'll see a waning gibbous ball, then a third quarter ball and a waning crescent ball. Finally, after one complete spin, you'll be back to new ball.

The phases of the Moon work the same way. We see new moon when the Moon lies in the same direction from Earth as the Sun and full moon when it lies in the opposite direction. We see the other phases in between, as the Moon slowly orbits the Earth about once each month.

Challenge: When we see new moon, what phase of Earth would be seen by people on the Moon? (For the answer, visit www.BigKidScience.com.)

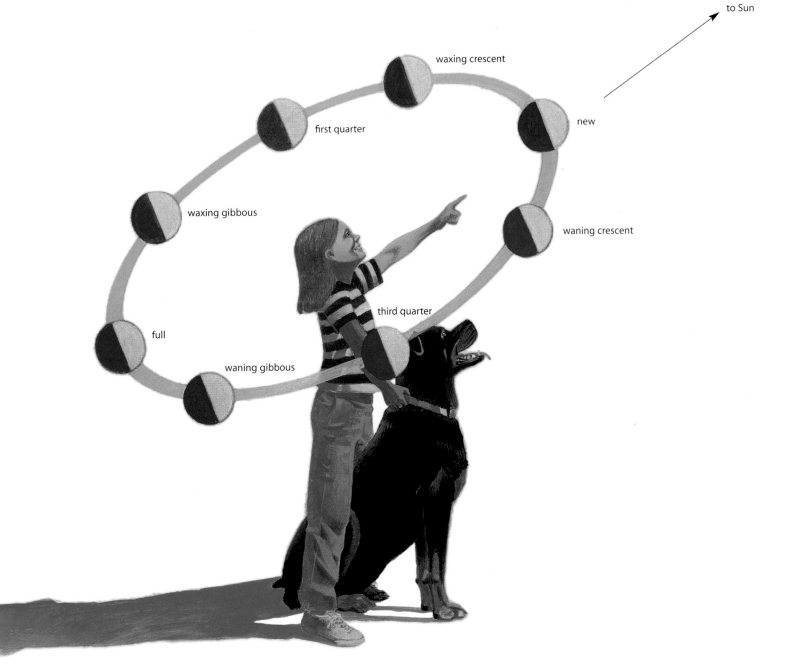

About the Author

Jeffrey Bennett is a Colorado-based astrophysicist and former NASA scientist, as well as Max's "dad." He has written college textbooks on mathematics, statistics, astronomy, and astrobiology, in addition to his books for children and the general public. He also proposed and helped develop the Voyage scale model solar system on the National Mall in Washington, DC.

About Max

The real Max is a 120-pound (55-kilogram) Rottweiler who lives in Colorado. His playful antics provided the inspiration for this book. Max is best-known for his merry-go-round trick, in which he makes a playground merry-go-round spin by running around it while pushing on it with his paws. Once it is spinning fast, he jumps on and off—always careful not to bang into any children riding with him. He's also the only dog we know who won't eat a steak unless you first cut it into small pieces for him.

About the Artist

Alan Okamoto was born in 1957, at the "Birth of the Space Age." His mother claims to have purposefully sculpted his head to be as round as a "perfect space helmet." His father was a farmer and civil engineer who rode his trusty tractor while wearing what Alan understood to be a spacesuit. On weekends, Alan and his siblings would explore the California Central Valley countryside, where they farmed and played in the mud. Exploring opened their minds to nature, as they exercised their imaginations and observations. Alan holds a BFA in commercial illustration.

Photo by Valari Jack

All Big Kid Science books are written and reviewed by real scientists, so you can trust them to be both fun and scientifically accurate. To learn more about Big Kid Science books and educational products, be sure to visit us at
www.BigKidScience.com